10 for dinner

Jo Ellen Bogart

Illustrations by Carlos Freire

Scholastic
Toronto • Sydney • New York • London • Auckland

Scholastic-TAB Publications Ltd.
123 Newkirk Road, Richmond Hill, Ontario, Canada L4C 3G5

Scholastic Inc.
730 Broadway, New York, NY 10003, USA

Ashton Scholastic Pty Limited
PO Box 579, Gosford, NSW 2250, Australia

Ashton Scholastic Limited
165 Marua Road, Panmure, Auckland, New Zealand

Scholastic Publications Ltd.
Holly Walk, Leamington Spa, Warwickshire, CV32 4LS England

30 29   5 6 / 0

Printed in the U.S.A.   08

Canadian Cataloguing in Publication Data

Bogart, Jo Ellen, 1945-
  10 for dinner

Issued also in French under title: 10 à la fête.
ISBN 0-590-71949-1 (little book)

I. Freire, Carlos, 1943-   . II. Title.
PS8553.064T45 1989b   jC813'.54   C88-095360-8
PZ7.B64Te 1989b

To my children, Adam and Jill
Jo Ellen Bogart

To Pacha and to Beto
Carlos Freire

Margo invited 10 friends for dinner on her birthday.

She made 10 invitations and drew pictures of dogs and balloons on each one.

3

On the day of the party
5 guests came right on time
at 5 o'clock,

2 came at 5:10,

and 2 came at 5:15.

But 1 guest arrived
early — at a quarter to 4.

Margo's guests wore their party clothes.
3 guests wore T-shirts and shorts,
1 guest wore a pink lace dress,
2 wore jeans and western shirts,

and 3 wore jogging suits.

But 1 guest wore his Halloween costume.

Margo served macaroni and cheese, meatballs, carrot and raisin salad, celery sticks and watermelon.

6 guests tried some of everything,
2 guests just had meatballs and watermelon,

and 1 had macaroni and cheese and celery sticks.

But 1 guest asked for
a peanut butter sandwich with olives and sauerkraut.

Margo gave her guests colored paper to make hats.

2 guests made firefighter helmets,

1 made a surgeon's cap,

1 made a pirate hat,

2 made cowboy hats

and 3 made hats for clowns.

But 1 guest made a hat like the Loch Ness monster.

Margo asked her guests what they would like to sing.

2 said:

3 said:

3 said:

Margo asked her guests what they would like to play.

1 guest said:

4 said:

14

Margo opened her presents.
2 guests gave her paperback books,
2 gave her fancy socks,
1 gave her an extra-long jumprope,
1 gave her left-handed scissors,
2 gave her hats,
and 1 gave her
a harmonica.

But 1 guest brought a big red box with a black bow.
Inside was a huge rock
with a shell fossil.

When the party was over,
5 guests went home in cars,
2 rode home on their bikes,

and 2 went on foot.

But 1 guest stayed to help with the dishes.